Copyright © 1972 by Roger Duvoisin
ISBN 0 370 01145 7
Printed in Great Britain for
The Bodley Head Ltd
9 Bow Street, London WC2
by William Clowes & Sons Ltd, Beccles
Colour separations by Colourcraftsmen Ltd, Chelmsford
First published 1972

The Crocodile in the Tree

Roger Duvoisin

The Bodley Head

LONDON · SYDNEY · TORONTO

Bertha the duck and
Johnny the rabbit were
sitting under the old
oak when Johnny,
looking up, cried
suddenly,

"Bertha, I just saw
a crocodile's tail stick-
ing out of that hole up
there in the trunk."

"Don't worry,
Johnny, we all see
things at times."

"I said I SAW A CROCODILE'S TAIL," cried Johnny, "and I will not stay here another moment. Good-bye."

"Good morning, Bertha," said a voice behind the duck.

In one jump Bertha turned round and came face to face with a crocodile's head sticking out of a bottom hole in the trunk.

"Please, Bertha," said the crocodile's head, "stay a while so we can talk a bit. Have no fear, I wouldn't think of eating you up."

The crocodile's head opened its long, long mouth in a laugh which showed four long, long rows of teeth.

"What are you?" asked Bertha. "A crocodile or just a crocodile's head?"

"A whole crocodile," answered the crocodile's head. "The rest of me is up there inside the trunk. Not comfortable, I dare say."

"Where do you come from?" asked Bertha.

"That's unimportant. I am here, that's what counts. I live in this hollow tree during the day and go out at night to lie down on the grass, look at the moon, and swim in the pond. I miss the sun. Fancy a crocodile unable to doze in the sun! My green colour will fade and I will look like an unripe apple. And I do miss flowers so."

"Then, why do you stay in that tree with your tail up?"

"I must hide because everyone is afraid of crocodiles on account of their many teeth. Silly, isn't it? If your farmer sees me he might fetch his gun and, BOOM, that would be the end of me. That would be sad if you consider that I still have a good four hundred years to live. If people only knew there are GOOD crocodiles."

"Poor crocodile," said Bertha. "I will not leave you here. Up in our barn there are comfortable hiding places where you will not have to live with your tail up. Come, I will introduce you to the barnyard. And do not fear Mr. Sweetpeas, the farmer. He and his wife have gone to the market."

What a din the crocodile started when he entered the barnyard with Bertha. The horses and the cows reared and kicked; the sheep and the pig ran under the chicken house; the goat jumped on to the tractor; the hens, the ducks, flew to the top of the barn with the pigeons, and Coco the dog barked until he was hoarse.

"You see, Bertha, that's what I said," moaned the crocodile. "I frighten them all and I'm not even showing my teeth."

"Stop barking at my crocodile," said Bertha to Coco.

"A dog is to bark," answered Coco. "If I didn't bark who would?"
But Coco finally smelled the crocodile all along his length and said
he was all right. Then he went to chew on an old bone.

Seeing this, all the animals stopped kicking, shrieking, crowing,
bleating and came to look at the crocodile.

"My friend will live with us," explained Bertha. "You will love him, for he is kind and his rows of teeth are only to smile."

"That's all very well," said Carrot the cat. "I like him but what about Mr. and Mrs. Sweetpeas?"

"We will hide my crocodile in the barn until we can show Mr. Sweetpeas that he is a GOOD crocodile," said Bertha.

Everyone worked so hard to hide the crocodile in a cosy bed of straw that he was moved to tears.

"Believe me, my friends, they are *good* crocodile's tears," he said, wiping his eyes with Mr. Sweetpeas' old blue jeans.

Bertha was like a mother to her crocodile. She fed him, she tucked him in at night, she warned him when the farmer or his wife came to the barnyard so he could slip under the hay.

All went well until, one day, Mrs. Sweetpeas burst into the barn to fetch some apples as Bertha and Coco were chatting with the crocodile. Coco had barely time to pull some hay over the crocodile and Bertha to sit on his head with her wings spread out.

"What are you doing here, Bertha?" asked Mrs. Sweetpeas. "Laying eggs where you shouldn't? Let me see."

She pushed Bertha aside and there was the crocodile's head.

"Oh, hello," said the crocodile with his sweetest smile.

"A CROCODILE! A CROCODILE!" screamed Mrs. Sweetpeas and ran out of the barn to the farmhouse.

"There is a crocodile in the barn and the duck was sitting on its head!" she cried out to Mr. Sweetpeas.

"What are you saying?" asked her husband.

"I SAID BERTHA WAS SITTING ON A CROCODILE'S HEAD!"

"Are you right in your mind, dear?"

"I know what I see and *I saw* Bertha on a crocodile's head. Go and see for yourself. That is, if you are not afraid of crocodiles."

So, Mr. Sweetpeas went to see.

In the meantime, in the barn, the animals worried about their crocodile. He could not, in daylight, go back to his tree trunk.

"The police will come," said Bertha, "and they will take our crocodile to the zoo."

"Or kill it," said Carrot the cat.

"I have an idea," said Coco. "There is a big loose board behind the hay no one but me knows about. I found it one day running after a rat. That's where I hide my bones. Fine place for a crocodile."

The crocodile slipped under the board to hide in the space below while Coco pushed some hay over it.

"Watch out," cried Bertha. "Here comes Mr. Sweetpeas. Everyone to his own affairs and please look innocent."

Mr. Sweetpeas looked around and behind and under everything in the barnyard but there was no crocodile. He called Coco.

"Come, Coco, smell, smell the crocodile!"

Coco wagged his tail and ran everywhere, barking loudly. Then he went to sleep in his kennel as if he could not care less about crocodiles.

"I knew there was no crocodile," said Mr. Sweetpeas. "I wonder what ailed Marguerite?" And he returned to the farmhouse.

All the animals were full of joy and embraced each other. All except the crocodile. He looked sad when he came out from under the barn floor.

"I am so heart-broken that I have scared the farmer's wife," he sighed. "She seems such a sweet lady. I already like her very much."

"She *is* nice," said Carrot. "She loves us so much and takes such good care of us."

"And how she loves flowers," added Bertha. "Most of the day one can see her bending down over her flower borders picking out weeds and planting new flowers. Her garden is beautiful."

"I adore flowers too," sighed the crocodile, "but I can never see them for I must hide during the day. Alas, the farmer's wife and I could be such good friends. We have so much in common!"

During the night, the crocodile thought much about the good farmer's wife and he said to himself,

"If I could only let her know how much I love her!"

Then he smiled with all his teeth. He knew what to do. At dawn, before the farmers were up, he went to the meadow to pick a beautiful bouquet of white daisies mixed with lovely wild grasses. He took it to the farmhouse porch and placed it on the little table on which Mrs. Sweetpeas served breakfast on sunny days.

How delighted was Mrs. Sweetpeas when she saw the bouquet.

"Oh, darling," she said to her husband, "it is nice and thoughtful of you to pick these daisies for me."

"I did not pick them," protested Mr. Sweetpeas.

"Then who did?" she wondered.

"That's what I would like to know," answered the farmer.

The next morning the crocodile brought to the little table a big bunch of blue bergamots set among wild ferns. It was so beautiful that it brought smiles of joy to Mrs. Sweetpeas' face.

Then the next morning, the crocodile made a bouquet of brown-eyed Susans which he picked at the edge of the wood.

Then it was a bouquet of tall loosestrifes which grew beyond the pond. Their purple colours were as fresh as the morning sky.

Mrs. Sweetpeas was happier and happier to see these lovely flowers although she could not guess who was picking them.

"We must find who brings these bouquets for you," declared Mr. Sweetpeas. "We must."

The next morning before dawn Mr. and Mrs. Sweetpeas went down to the living room to watch from behind the porch door. There were no flowers yet on the breakfast table. But, suddenly, the crocodile appeared with a brilliant bouquet of the wild cardinal flowers which grew beside the stream.

"Well," exclaimed the farmer. "So there *was* a crocodile in the barn after all! And, my dear, what a considerate crocodile!"

"Such a darling crocodile," exclaimed Mrs. Sweetpeas. "He is an artist with flowers and he loves them as much as I do."

She ran to the crocodile to pat him and to thank him for all the

lovely bouquets while Mr. Sweetpeas shook his paw.

All the animals on the farm, led by Bertha, Coco and Carrot, came running to join in the rejoicing.

From then on there were three to care for the farm flower garden,
Mrs. Sweetpeas, the crocodile, and Bertha. Never again did the crocodile have to hide under the barn floor or in the tree.

"Life becomes so beautiful when we find a friend with whom we
have much in common," mused the crocodile.